Three Young Pilgrims

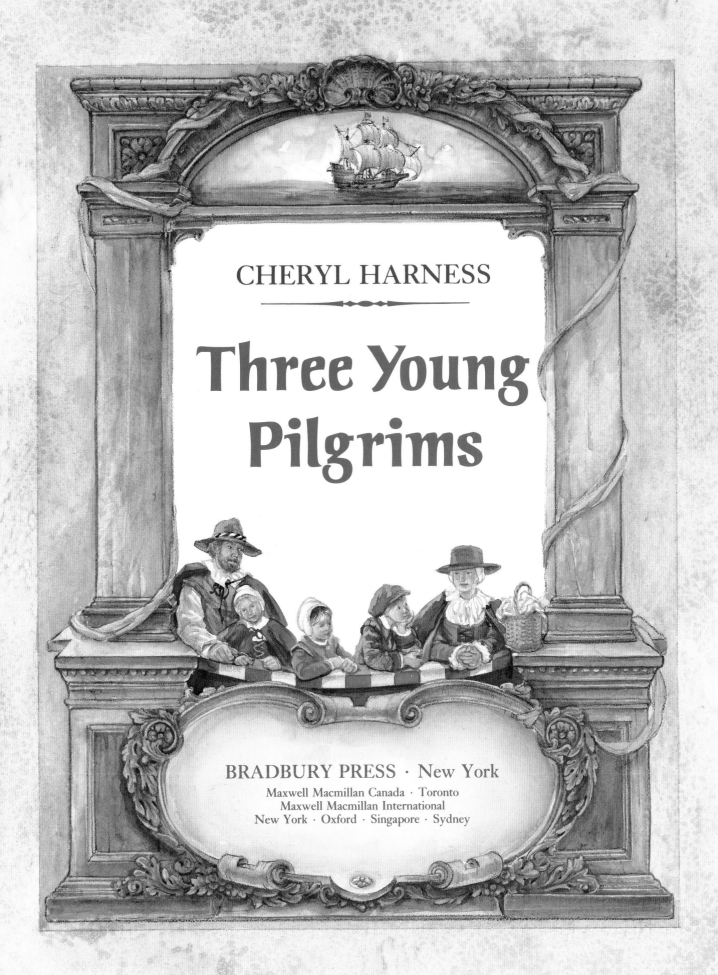

CHERYL HARNESS

Three Young Pilgrims

BRADBURY PRESS · New York

Maxwell Macmillan Canada · Toronto
Maxwell Macmillan International
New York · Oxford · Singapore · Sydney

ACKNOWLEDGMENTS
I wish to acknowledge the life and writings of William Bradford,
the support of Barbara Lalicki, who edited this book,
and the inspiration and assistance provided by
the staff of Plimoth Plantation.

Bradbury Press
Macmillan Publishing Company
866 Third Avenue
New York, NY 10022

Maxwell Macmillan Canada, Inc.
1200 Eglinton Avenue East
Suite 200
Don Mills, Ontario M3C 3N1

Macmillan Publishing Company is part of the Maxwell Communication
Group of Companies.

First American edition
Printed and bound in Hong Kong by South China Printing Company (1988) Ltd.
10   9   8   7   6   5   4
The text of this book is set in Janson
Typography by Julie Quan

LIBRARY OF CONGRESS CATALOGING-IN-PUBLICATION DATA

Harness, Cheryl.
Three young pilgrims / written and illustrated by Cheryl Harness.
—1st American ed.
p.   cm.
Summary: Mary, Remember, and Bartholomew are among the pilgrims
who survive the harsh early years in America and see New Plymouth
grow into a prosperous colony.
ISBN 0-02-742643-2
1. Pilgrims (New Plymouth Colony)—Juvenile fiction.
[1. Pilgrims (New Plymouth Colony)—Fiction.   2. Massachusetts—
History—New Plymouth, 1620–1691—Fiction.]   I. Title.
PZ7.H2277Th   1992
[Fic]—dc20   91-7289   CIP   AC

A NOTE ABOUT THE ART
The illustrations for *Three Young Pilgrims* were done on cold-pressed Strathmore
illustration board using a combination of watercolor, gouache and colored pencil.
They were color-separated by scanner and reproduced in four colors
using red, blue, yellow, and black inks.

Ten percent of the author's royalties for the work will be
donated to Plimoth Plantation.

To the Pilgrims

A Note from the Author

The purpose of this book is to tell part of the story of a family. The Allertons' adventures, during one year, between the autumns of 1620 and 1621, cannot be told apart from the larger story of a group of brave people who set out to make a new life in a land that was unknown to them.

The book is not meant to be a scholarly work on the Pilgrims. Much has been written in greater detail about their ways and wanderings. It is, instead, a storybook, an illustrated primer that will, perhaps, lead the reader to study further.

While researching this story I visited Plimoth Plantation in Plymouth, Massachusetts. This living history museum strives to give an authentic simulation of how life was lived in the 1620s. It's a trip I would recommend to anyone who wants to discover more.

HUDSON
BAY

CANADA

200 m.

GULF OF
ST. LAWRENCE

NEWFOUNDLAND

Prince
Edward
Island

Oceanus Hopkins
born at sea

WEST

NOVA SCOTIA

Plymouth

Cape Cod
First landfall of
the Mayflower
November 9, 1620

The Pilgrims
landed at Plymouth
December 18, 1620

Jamestown

ATLANTIC OCEAN

CUBA

SOUTH

NORTH

SCOTLAND

GLASGOW

William Bradford and William Brewster fled from their homes in Scrooby to Holland in 1608.

IRELAND

DUBLIN

SCROOBY

AMSTERDAM

LONDON

LEIDEN
The Saints left for England August 1, 1620

September 6, 1620 the Mayflower and 102 Pilgrims, 30 crew left Plymouth harbor and sailed off alone.

Southampton

Plymouth

English Channel

aboard the Speedwell

The Mayflower and her sister ship, the Speedwell left Southampton on the 5th of August. The leaky Speedwell was forced to turn back.

PARIS

FRANCE

William Butten dies at sea

The Bay of Biscay

SPAIN

PORTUGAL

MADRID

AZORES ISLANDS

LISBON

MEDITERRANEAN SEA

EAST

CASABLANCA

Mary, Remember, and Bartholomew stood on the deck of a little boat in the very middle of dark blue ocean all around. They watched for mermaids and whales, pirates, and, most of all, land.

AFRICA

Down below their feet were the dark, bad-smelling rooms for the people and their bundles. Below them was the hold full of cargo and barrels of food and water. Below all this was dark, cold seawater where Mama said fish swam through the bones of poor drowned sailors.

Main·topsail

Mizzen

Main Course

Master Christopher Jones

Main Mast

Poop Deck

Mizzen mast

Chart room

Mr. Coppin is the PILOT

Half Deck

Great Cabin

Steerage

Binnacle is where the compass is kept

Capstan

Tiller

Whipstaff

Cannon

'Tween Decks

Food and Baggage

Barrels of Beer

Casks of Water

Rudder

Rocks for Ballast

Keel

Fore-topsail

Forecourse

Spritsail

Longboat

Firebox for cooking

Forecastle the crew sleeps here

Hatch

Beak

Anchor windlass

Pigs and Goats kept in crates

Anchor lines

It had been sixty days since the ship sailed from England.
Finally, one cold November morning, there was a shouting:
"*Land!* Land ho! 'Tis America!"

The Pilgrims strained to see a pale ribbon of land.

Every morning the thin line on the horizon was thicker.
Mary wondered if bears were watching from behind the
tiny trees.

Captain Jones told the sailors to drop the *Mayflower*'s iron
anchor into the sea.

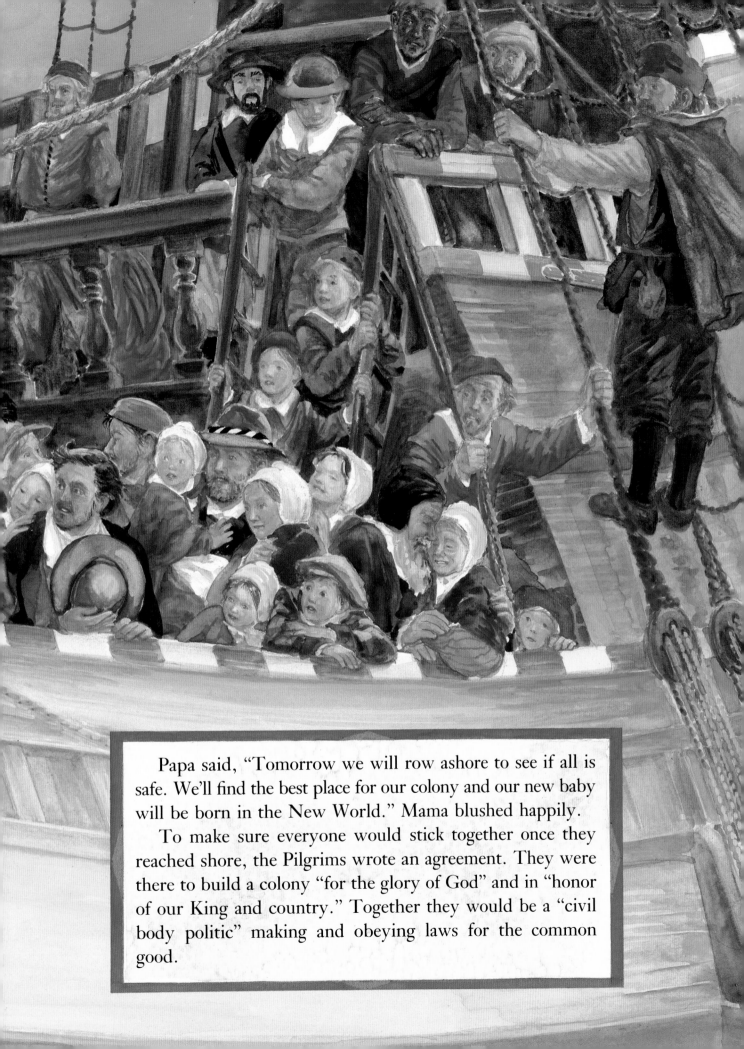

Papa said, "Tomorrow we will row ashore to see if all is safe. We'll find the best place for our colony and our new baby will be born in the New World." Mama blushed happily.

To make sure everyone would stick together once they reached shore, the Pilgrims wrote an agreement. They were there to build a colony "for the glory of God" and in "honor of our King and country." Together they would be a "civil body politic" making and obeying laws for the common good.

It was scary getting into the little boat. Everyone's legs were wobbly after so many weeks at sea. But then, how wonderful to run on the solid land!

Mama and the other women washed their families' clothes in the water and spread them out to dry on the rocks and bushes. The children went exploring. "Don't go off too far," the mothers called.

Mary thought she saw a face peeking from behind a rock, but when she looked there was no one there.

That afternoon the Pilgrims returned to the *Mayflower*. It would be their shelter until the place to settle was found. It was an important decision.

Finally, just before Christmas, Papa said to Mama, "We found a fine place to build. We will call it Plymouth Colony."

Mama smiled. "I'm glad, Isaac."

The children saw that her face was thin and pale. They felt worried. Everyone was hungry and tired of living crowded together on the damp, smelly ship. On the land and on the gray, rolling sea, the days and nights were growing cold and bitter.

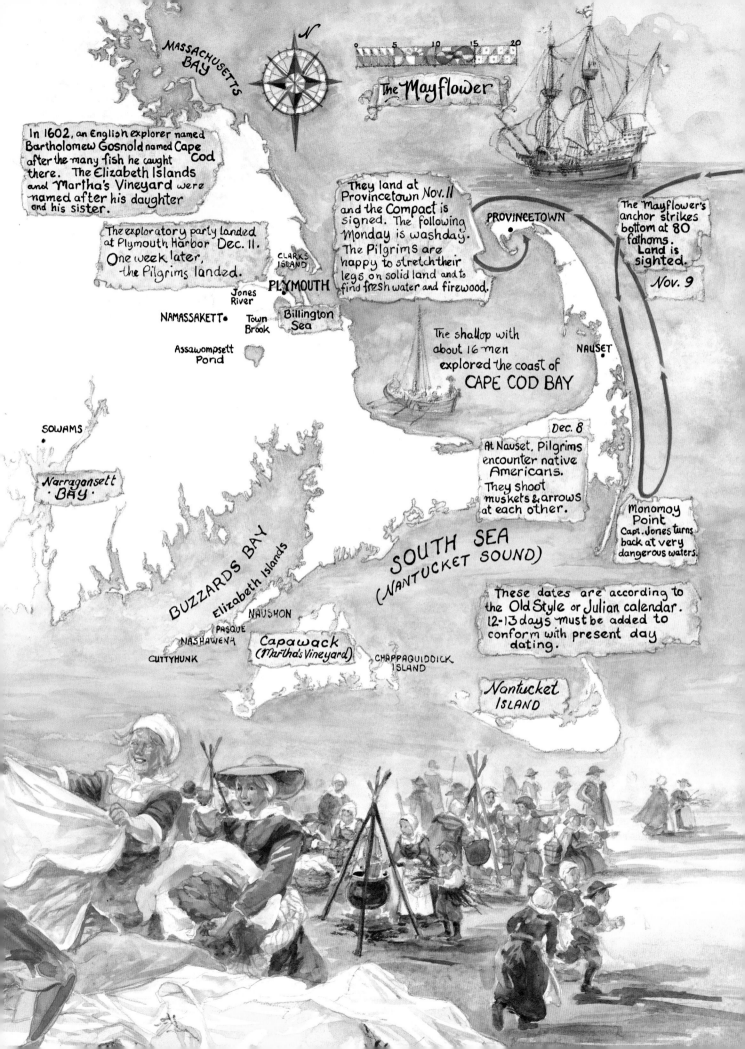

MASSACHUSETTS BAY

N

5 10 15 20

The Mayflower

In 1602, an English explorer named Bartholomew Gosnold named Cape Cod after the many fish he caught there. The Elizabeth Islands and Martha's Vineyard were named after his daughter and his sister.

They land at Provincetown Nov. 11 and the Compact is signed. The following Monday is washday. The Pilgrims are happy to stretch their legs on solid land and to find fresh water and firewood.

PROVINCETOWN

The Mayflower's anchor strikes bottom at 80 fathoms. Land is sighted. Nov. 9

The exploratory party landed at Plymouth Harbor Dec. 11. One week later, the Pilgrims landed.

CLARKS ISLAND

PLYMOUTH

Jones River

NAMASSAKETT•

Town Brook

Billington Sea

Assawompsett Pond

The shallop with about 16 men explored the coast of CAPE COD BAY

NAUSET

SOWAMS

Narragansett BAY

Dec. 8

At Nauset, Pilgrims encounter native Americans. They shoot muskets & arrows at each other.

Monomoy Point Capt. Jones turns back at very dangerous waters.

BUZZARDS BAY

Elizabeth Islands

SOUTH SEA (NANTUCKET SOUND)

NAUSHON

PASQUE

NASHAWENA

CUTTYHUNK

Capawack (Martha's Vineyard)

CHAPPAQUIDDICK ISLAND

These dates are according to the Old Style or Julian calendar. 12-13 days must be added to conform with present day dating.

Nantucket ISLAND

Mary watched snowflakes melt into the salty sea. She could hear the ringing of axes and pounding of hammers. The sounds carried clearly across the water from the land where Papa and the others were building shelter as fast as they could.

Some of the grown-ups were beginning to be sick. Mistress Mullins had died of the sickness. Mr. Bradford's sad, silent wife had fallen into the sea and drowned. Mary shivered and wished that the new baby would come, that spring would come, and that they could all be warm and safe together in their own house with supper in the kettle.

In the next weeks, those who were strong enough moved
their belongings from the ship to the Common House and
to their own half-built houses. One dark winter evening, Papa
built a smoky fire in their own hearth. That night, Bartholomew, Remember, and Mary warmed their fingers with their
whispered prayers and bundled up with him and Mama. The
family listened long to the sounds of the woods before falling
asleep, and the wind blew cold off the sea.

On the sixteenth day of March, Mary found tiny spring flowers in a clump of melting snow.

Remember said, "It must be spring. Mama said, 'Winter is most dark and cold just before spring.'"

In the darkest winter, half of the Pilgrims had died of the Great Sickness. Mama and the new baby died, too. A tear slipped down Bartholomew's nose. Then he saw the Indian.

He stood quietly at the edge of the woods and looked at them with keen dark eyes. His skin was the color of copper. The children turned and ran to find Papa.

They found him trying to break up the rocky soil of their garden.

"Papa, come with us!"

"Not now . . ." he began in a weary voice.

They pulled his hands. "There's an Indian!"

They saw the tall man walk up to Mr. Hopkins and Mr. Bradford.

"Welcome, Englishmen!" he said in a loud, deep voice. "My name is Samoset."

The thin, sad Pilgrims came out of their fields and doorways to see the Indian. After spending the night with the Hopkins family, Samoset went back to his home in the forest.

When he came back, he brought his friend Squanto with him. They brought food and later showed the settlers how to plant corn a new way. In each hill of corn they buried small fish.

Remember planted the herbs and
flowers Mama had brought.
When no one was looking,
Mary planted a fish, too.

On a pearly April morning, Captain Jones sailed away on the *Mayflower* back to the Old World. Many of the Pilgrims wiped away homesick tears. When the ship was a glint on the horizon, they walked back to their work. This was home now.

All down the warm, green summer days everyone tended their gardens and crops in the fields. The corn stood taller than Mary could reach. When Priscilla Mullins and John Alden were married, Remember brought primroses from Mama's garden. "That fish must have helped." Mary smiled to herself.

There was going to be a rich harvest. Well into the cool, blue evenings, the Pilgrims worked gathering in the squash, peas, beans, barley, and corn. Herbs for medicines and seasonings were tied into sweet-smelling bunches.

After the Sabbath prayers and hymn singing, Governor Bradford stood before the congregation. His collar was very white beneath his sunburned face.

"We will invite our Indian brothers to feast with us and offer prayers of thanksgiving to the Maker for a bountiful harvest."

It would be a fine thing to do. Nobody had forgotten how it felt to be cold and hungry.

For days Plymouth was filled with the good smells of cooking. A company of men had been sent to the Indian village with the invitation to the feast. Massasoit, the great leader, Samoset, Squanto, and nearly ninety other men emerged from the shadowy woods wearing feathers in their black hair. The feasting went on for three days. As the deer brought by the Indians roasted and food was set out on long tables, the men challenged each other to see who was strongest, whose feet ran fastest.

Late at night, Papa and his children sat at the edge of the circle of firelight. There was singing, and far off they could see the harvest moon rising out of the ocean. The moonpath of light might have led all the way back to the old homes in Holland and England. Mary sat in Papa's lap munching a bit of berry tart.

Bartholomew asked, "Papa, are you happy we came to America?"

Remember frowned at her brother. She didn't want Papa to be sad. Mary looked up into Papa's dark eyes.

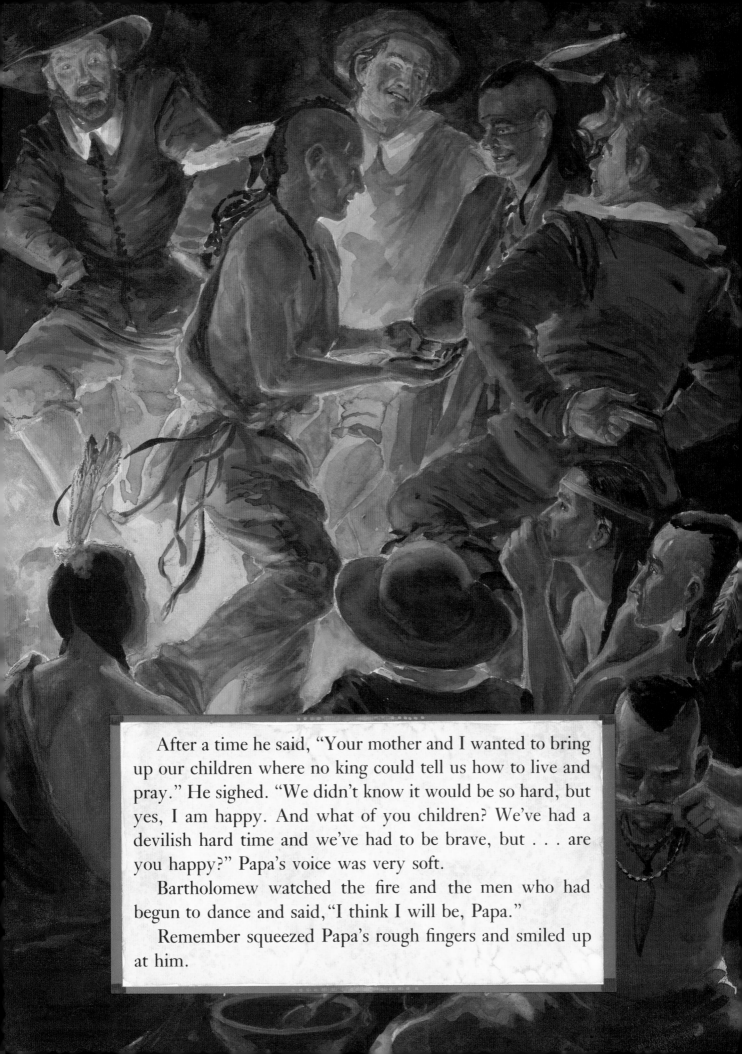

After a time he said, "Your mother and I wanted to bring up our children where no king could tell us how to live and pray." He sighed. "We didn't know it would be so hard, but yes, I am happy. And what of you children? We've had a devilish hard time and we've had to be brave, but . . . are you happy?" Papa's voice was very soft.

Bartholomew watched the fire and the men who had begun to dance and said, "I think I will be, Papa."

Remember squeezed Papa's rough fingers and smiled up at him.

Mary wished that Mama were there. Papa's arms tightened around her. Feeling warm and safe, she whispered, "I wasn't happy." Papa's soft whiskers brushed her cheek.

The four of them listened to the singing and the sea. Way past bedtime, away from the fire, the moon lighted the paths leading home.

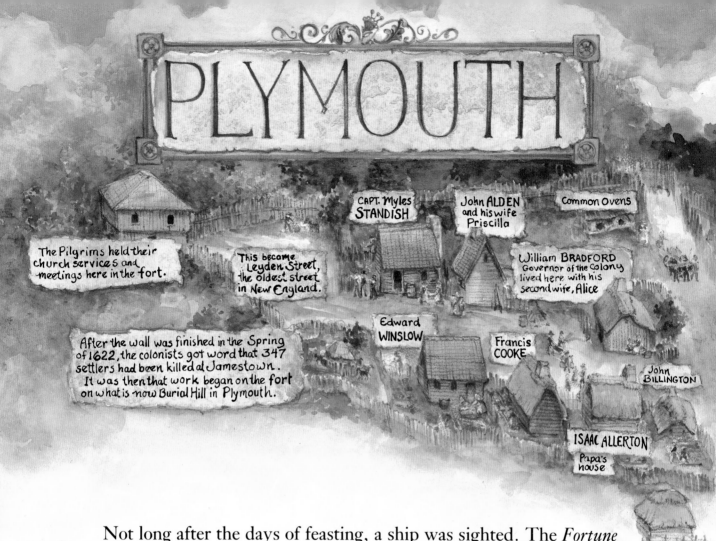

PLYMOUTH

The Pilgrims held their church services and meetings here in the fort.

This become Leyden Street, the oldest street in New England.

CAPT. Myles STANDISH

John ALDEN and his wife Priscilla

Common Ovens

William BRADFORD Governor of the colony lived here with his second wife, Alice

Edward WINSLOW

Francis COOKE

John BILLINGTON

After the wall was finished in the Spring of 1622, the colonists got word that 347 settlers had been killed at Jamestown. It was then that work began on the fort on what is now Burial Hill in Plymouth.

ISAAC ALLERTON

Papa's house

Not long after the days of feasting, a ship was sighted. The *Fortune* brought thirty-five new settlers and no food to feed them. There followed a hungry winter and more hard times. The Pilgrims' good friend Squanto died in September of 1622. The next summer a miraculous rain came just in time to save the harvest, and two more ships came from England: the *Anne* and the *Little James*. Many families were reunited. Deacon Fuller's wife and Elder Brewster's daughters were aboard. Two years later, Fear Brewster became Papa's second wife.

Slowly the hungry years passed, and the colony grew as the land became prosperous. The Pilgrims and their children moved to their own farms in newly created townships such as Rehoboth and Duxbury.

1002 Leif Ericsson sails to the New World

1492 Christopher Columbus discovers Hispanola and Cuba

1497 John Cabot lands at Nova Scotia

1521 Cortes takes Mexico City from the Aztecs

1534 Jacques Cartier sails to Canada

1541 Hernando DeSoto crosses the Mississippi River

1587 Virginia Dare born at Roanoke

Earlier voyages and explorations in the "NEW WORLD"

1602 Bartholomew Gosnold names Cape Cod

1607 Jamestown Colony is founded in Virginia

1608 Samuel de Champlain establishes a French colony at Quebec

Seven houses were built the first Spring and Summer after the dreadful Winter of the Great Sickness. By 1627 over 150 people lived in Plymouth Colony.

By trading cattle, corn, beaver pelts and lumber, the Pilgrims, in 1645, finally paid off their terrible debts to the money lenders in London who had financed the adventure. Nearly 45 years later, King William III made Plymouth a part of the Colony of Massachusetts Bay.

Stephen HOPKINS

John HOWLAND

Dr. Samuel FULLER

Richard WARREN

George SOULE

To the SEA

William & Mary BREWSTER

Peter BROWNE

Tom PRENCE

Common houses where food was stored

When Bartholomew grew up, he went back to England. Remember got married and moved to Salem. Mary became the wife of Tom Cushman, who had come over on the *Fortune*. They had eight children, and when Mary Allerton Cushman died in 1699, the last passenger of the *Mayflower* passed from the earth.

Around the time of the
PILGRIMS

In the sea to the north of AFRICA you would find Barbary Pirates.

Way to the south the kingdom of Kongo was growing weak from the slave traders of Portugal.

The fierce SHOGUN of JAPAN was driving out the European missionaries of Christianity. He was afraid they would bring European soldiers.

In England the plays of William Shakespeare were being published. Dr. Harvey was finding out how blood circulates in people's bodies.

Opera was being invented in where Galileo Italy had discovered 4 moons of Jupiter.

A war had begun in GERMANY that would last 30 years.

The Ming dynasty of emperors was beginning in CHINA

The first of the Romanov czars ruled RUSSIA The Cossacks ruled the Ukraine.

INDIA Work would soon begin on the • To the east in the TAJ MAHAL BAY of BENGAL Holland, Portugal and England were fighting for control of the buying and selling of ginger and cinnamon.

Rembrandt was painting in HOLLAND Louis XIII sat on the throne of *France*. It was the time of the Three Musketeers.

Popham

1608 English colonists at Sagadahoc at the Kennebec River decide to go home.

1609 Henry Hudson on an expedition for the Dutch East India Company, sails his ship, the Half Moon into Hudson Bay

1614

Pocahontus marries John Rolfe

Captain John Smith explores New England

In 1616 his book about the journey is published in London

Thomas Hunt kidnaps Squanto

1620 Captain Thomas Dermer comes to Capawack Island

THE SAINTS

LEYDEN

In the days of the Pilgrims, the church of the king was the church of the nation, so King James's church was the Church of England. Some folks thought that the king's church should be stricter, pure and plain. Some even left it altogether. This was against the law. Even though they loved England, these people were in too much trouble to stay so they went to Holland and settled in the town of Leyden.

When the Mayflower reached Plymouth Colony, Susanna White had a baby boy. He was named Peregrine which meant "traveler".

+Thomas Rogers +Moses Fletcher Edward and +Elizabeth Winslow +William and Susanna White Francis Cooke +John Turner +Tom Tinker +his wife +and son +Edward and Anne Tilley

George Soule +Degory Priest

+John Crackstone

+William Batten Sam Fuller's servant boy, died on the voyage to America.

+Joseph Rogers +John Crackstone, Jr

Dr Samuel Fuller

+Ellen More Ellen and her brothers, Richard and Jasper, were orphans. In these days, it was common for orphans to be bound to a family as servants. They'd be released when they turned 21.

++two Turner boys John Cooke

Humility Cooper Henry Samson two young cousins of Mr. & Mrs. Tilley

William Brewster, his wife, Mary, and young William Bradford, who later became the governor of Plymouth, were among them.

After twelve years in Holland, they and other members of their little church decided to go to America, where there was lots of land and greater freedom.

Because they thought of themselves as God's chosen people, they called themselves Saints. The others who sailed were Strangers to them, so that's what they were called.

John Carver was a leader in the Pilgrims' church. In Plymouth, he was elected the first Governor of the colony. After he died in the summer of 1621, William Bradford was elected.

William Brewster had been the royal postmaster of Scrooby near Sherwood Forest. In Holland, he became a silk weaver and a printer. He printed religious pamphlets that made King James very angry all over again.

William Bradford was the Governor for thirty-three years. The book he wrote "Of Plymouth Plantation" tells us almost everything we know about the Pilgrims' adventure.

♣John and ♣Elizabeth Tilley

♣John Goodman

Isaac Allerton and his wife, ♣Mary

♣Roger Wilder

William Latham

Desire Minter

♣John and ♣Catherine Carver

John Howland

William and Mary Brewster

Patience Brewster married Elizabeth Tilley much later

William and ♣Dorothy Bradford

Fear Brewster

Mary Allerton was 4 years old

♣John Hooke a servant boy

Bartholomew (8) and Remember (6) Allerton

Wrestling Brewster His big brother's name was Love.

Richard and ♣Jasper More worked for the Brewsters and the Carvers.

John Bradford stayed behind. He was brought to the New World later on.

♣These people died before the first Thanksgiving.

Patience and Fear Brewster did not sail with their parents on the Mayflower. Three years later, they came to America aboard the Anne. Their brother Jonathan came too.

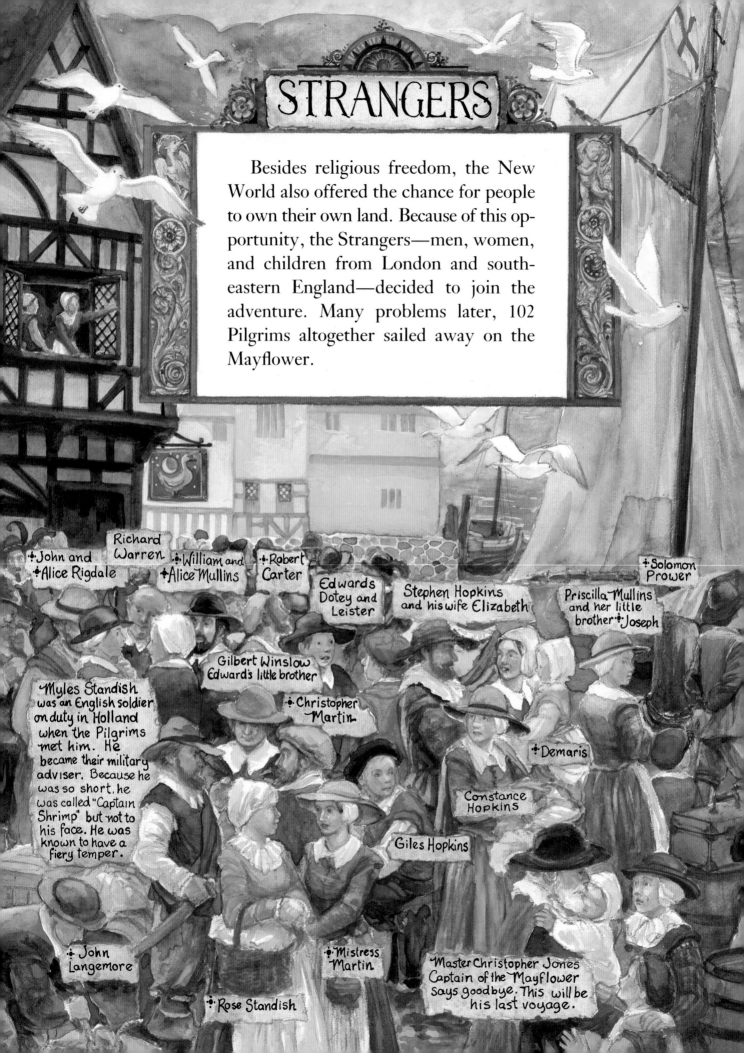

STRANGERS

Besides religious freedom, the New World also offered the chance for people to own their own land. Because of this opportunity, the Strangers—men, women, and children from London and southeastern England—decided to join the adventure. Many problems later, 102 Pilgrims altogether sailed away on the Mayflower.

Richard Warren

✛John and ✛Alice Rigdale

✛William and ✛Alice Mullins

✛Robert Carter

Edwards Dotey and Leister

Stephen Hopkins and his wife Elizabeth

✛Solomon Prower

Priscilla Mullins and her little brother ✛Joseph

Gilbert Winslow Edward's little brother

✛Christopher Martin

Myles Standish was an English soldier on duty in Holland when the Pilgrims met him. He became their military adviser. Because he was so short, he was called "Captain Shrimp" but not to his face. He was known to have a fiery temper.

✛Demaris

Constance Hopkins

Giles Hopkins

✛John Langemore

✛Mistress Martin

Master Christopher Jones Captain of the Mayflower says goodbye. This will be his last voyage.

✛Rose Standish

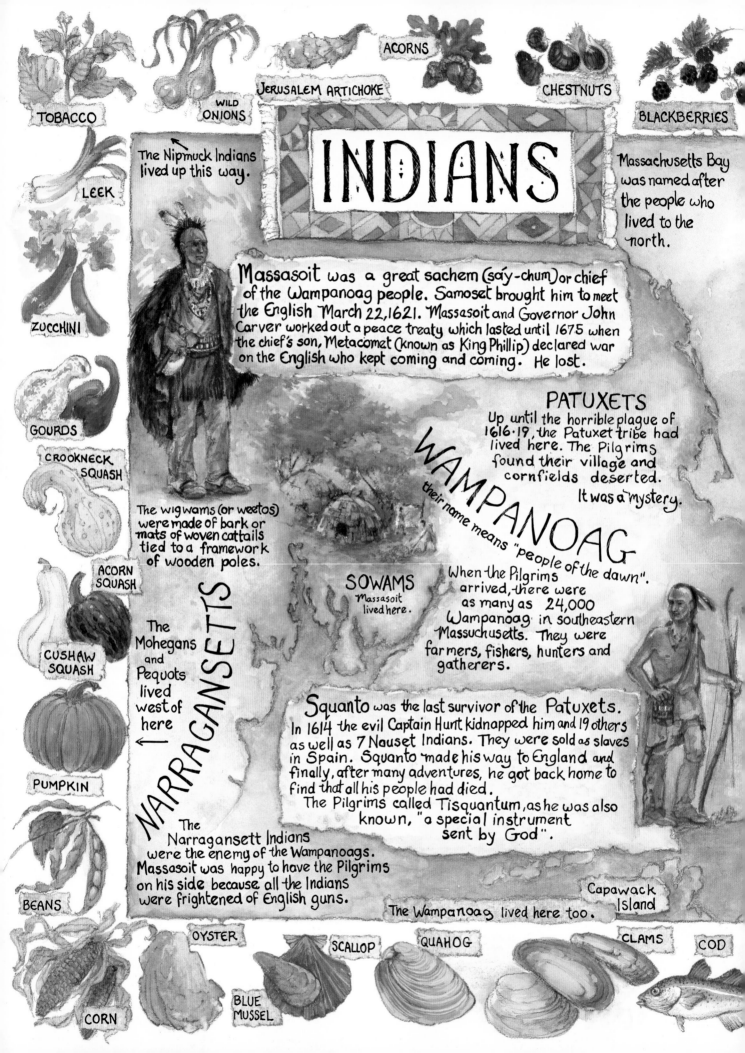

TOBACCO

WILD ONIONS

JERUSALEM ARTICHOKE

ACORNS

CHESTNUTS

BLACKBERRIES

LEEK

ZUCCHINI

GOURDS

CROOKNECK SQUASH

ACORN SQUASH

CUSHAW SQUASH

PUMPKIN

BEANS

CORN

OYSTER

BLUE MUSSEL

SCALLOP

QUAHOG

CLAMS

COD

INDIANS

The Nipmuck Indians lived up this way.

Massachusetts Bay was named after the people who lived to the north.

Massasoit was a great sachem (say-chum) or chief of the Wampanoag people. Samoset brought him to meet the English March 22, 1621. Massasoit and Governor John Carver worked out a peace treaty which lasted until 1675 when the chief's son, Metacomet (known as King Phillip) declared war on the English who kept coming and coming. He lost.

PATUXETS
Up until the horrible plague of 1616-19, the Patuxet tribe had lived here. The Pilgrims found their village and cornfields deserted.
It was a mystery.

WAMPANOAG
their name means "people of the dawn".

The wigwams (or weetos) were made of bark or mats of woven cattails tied to a framework of wooden poles.

SOWAMS
Massasoit lived here.

When the Pilgrims arrived, there were as many as 24,000 Wampanoag in southeastern Massachusetts. They were farmers, fishers, hunters and gatherers.

NARRAGANSETTS

The Mohegans and Pequots lived west of here

Squanto was the last survivor of the Patuxets. In 1614 the evil Captain Hunt kidnapped him and 19 others as well as 7 Nauset Indians. They were sold as slaves in Spain. Squanto made his way to England and finally, after many adventures, he got back home to find that all his people had died.
The Pilgrims called Tisquantum, as he was also known, "a special instrument sent by God".

The Narragansett Indians were the enemy of the Wampanoags. Massasoit was happy to have the Pilgrims on his side because all the Indians were frightened of English guns.

The Wampanoag lived here too.

Capawack Island

WILD CURRANTS

STRAWBERRIES and GOOSE BERRIES

GROUND NUTS

WALNUTS

CRABAPPLES

TURKEY

DUCK

GOOSE

When Samoset greeted the Pilgrims on the 16th of March, they were surprised that he spoke English. He learned it from sailors who had come to fish and trade near his home at Pemaquid Point way up north in Maine.

Samoset, an Algonkian chief, came south to Wampanoag lands with the English explorer, Capt. Thomas Dermer just 8 months before the Pilgrims arrived.

After watching the newcomers all winter, Massasoit asked Samoset to go say hello and see who these people were.

When the Englishmen were first exploring Cape Cod they found baskets of corn of all different colors buried in the sand. This corn belonged to the Nausets. William Bradford said it was "a very goodly sight, having never seen any such before." The Pilgrims borrowed some for seed. They paid it back.

WATER CRESS

CORN HILL

Later that evening, Bradford got caught in an Indian deer trap. The men laughed and laughed.

At the end of 1621, Canonicus, the sachem of the Narragansetts, sent a mysterious message to Governor Bradford: a rattlesnake skin full of arrows. The governor filled the snakeskin full of gunpowder and buckshot then sent it back. Things were quiet after that.

The first folks the Pilgrims met were from the Nauset tribe. These natives shot arrows at them.

LAMB'S QUARTERS

MAPLE SYRUP

BIRDS' EGGS

RACCOON

NAUSETS

Hobomok was one of the young leaders of Massasoit's tribe. He and Squanto stayed with the Pilgrims at Plymouth. They helped them in many ways. Squanto showed how to catch tasty eels. Hobomok helped the colonists' relations with the Nausets, the Narragansetts and the Massachusetts tribes.

Squanto's and Hobomok's friendship with the Pilgrims meant the survival of the colony.

BEAVER

Massasoit might have smoked a stone pipe that looked like this.

DEER

EEL

RABBIT   BEAR

HERRING

BLUEFISH

ALEWIFE

BIBLIOGRAPHY

*Anderson, Joan. *The First Thanksgiving Feast*. New York: Clarion, 1984.

*Beck, Barbara L. *The Pilgrims of Plymouth*. New York: Franklin Watts, 1972.

Bradford, William. *Of Plymouth Plantation, 1620–1647*. Edited by Samuel Eliot Morison. New York: Alfred A. Knopf, 1952.

Charlton, Warwick. *The Second Mayflower Adventure*. Boston: Little, Brown, 1957.

*Clapp, Patricia. *Constance*. New York: Viking Puffin, 1986.

*Colby, Jean Poindexter. *Plimoth Plantation, Then and Now*. New York: Hastings House, 1970.

Harris, John. *Saga of the Pilgrims*. Chester, CT: Globe Pequot, 1990.

*Rich, Louise Dickinson. *The First Book of the Early Settlers*. New York: Franklin Watts, 1959.

*Siegel, Beatrice. *A New Look at the Pilgrims: Why They Came to America*. New York: Walker, 1977.

**The Thanksgiving Primer*. A Plimoth Plantation Publication, 1987.

*Waters, Kate. *Sarah Morton's Day*. New York: Scholastic, 1989.

Weinstein-Farson, Laurie. *The Wampanoag*. New York: Chelsea House, 1988.

Wilbur, C. Keith. *The New England Indians*. Chester, CT: Globe Pequot, 1978.

*Books especially written for young readers